Race for Treasure

By Ace Landers
Illustrated by Dave White

SCHOLASTIC INC.

New York   Toronto   London   Auckland

Sydney   Mexico City   New Delhi   Hong Kong

ISBN 978-0-545-33454-9

HOT WHEELS and associated trademarks and trade dress are owned by, and used under
license from Mattel. Inc. © 2011 Mattel, Inc. All Rights Reserved.

Published by Scholastic Inc. SCHOLASTIC and associated logos
are trademarks and/or registered trademarks of Scholastic Inc.

Lexile® is a registered trademark of MetaMetrics.

12 11 10 9 8 7 6 5 4 3 2 1   11 12 13 14 15 16/0

Printed in the U.S.A.   40
First printing, October 2011

Today there is a race for treasure.

There are two teams.
The red team is ready to win.

So is the blue team.

The race is a relay. There are three legs.

Treasure is hidden in the caves. The team that finds it first will win.

Let the race begin!

The red team pulls in front.

But this is not a safe race!

There are pirate traps everywhere!

Both teams speed to the checkpoint.

Now the race goes down the mountain.

The blue team slides into first place.

The red team is close
behind them.

Watch out for the rockslide!

The blue team drives around the rocks. The red team rides over them.

There is a ramp ahead.
Who will get there first?

Both teams hit the ramp.

The blue team is still in the lead!

This is the last part of the race.

The racetrack splits. But which track leads to the treasure?

The blue cars each choose a track.

The red cars pick different tracks.

Each track leads
to a different cave!

One of the red cars hits a dead end!

The caves have many twists and turns.

The racers see a light
up ahead.

The light makes an *X* on the
ground. The *X* marks where
the treasure is hidden!

Which team will
win the treasure?

The red team wins!